A NARROW ESCAPE

The Lobster Chronicles 2

A NARROW ESCAPE

Jessica Scott Kerrin

Illustrations by
Shelagh Armstrong

Kids Can Press

To Jennifer of Roundy Rock Island — J.S.K.

Text © 2013 Jessica Scott Kerrin
Illustrations © 2013 Kids Can Press

This is a work of fiction and any resemblance of characters to persons living or dead is purely coincidental.

Kids Can Press acknowledges the financial support of the Government of Ontario, through the Ontario Media Development Corporation's Ontario Book Initiative; the Ontario Arts Council; the Canada Council for the Arts; and the Government of Canada, through the CBF, for our publishing activity.

Published in Canada by
Kids Can Press Ltd.
25 Dockside Drive
Toronto, ON M5A 0B5

Published in the U.S. by
Kids Can Press Ltd.
2250 Military Road
Tonawanda, NY 14150

www.kidscanpress.com

Edited by Sheila Barry
Designed by Marie Bartholomew
Illustrations by Shelagh Armstrong

This book is smyth sewn casebound.
Manufactured in Shen Zhen, Guang Dong, P.R. China, in 9/2012 by Printplus Limited

CM 13 0 9 8 7 6 5 4 3 2 1

Library and Archives Canada Cataloguing in Publication

Kerrin, Jessica Scott
   A narrow escape / written by Jessica Scott Kerrin ; illustrations by Shelagh Armstrong.

(The lobster chronicles)
ISBN 978-1-55453-642-9

I. Armstrong, Shelagh, 1961– II. Title. III. Series: Kerrin, Jessica Scott. The lobster chronicles.

PS8621.E77N37 2013   jC813>.6   C2012-904394-X

Kids Can Press is a ℓ℮ⓡ∪s™ Entertainment company

Contents

No Witnesses 7

List of Suspects 16

Lucky Catch 26

Accused 35

Deadly Aim 43

Marshy Hope 53

Decoy 62

Double-Cross 71

Interview 82

Tricked 92

Fiasco 102

Confession 112

Victory 119

Release 128

Acknowledgments 133

No Witnesses

When his teacher's cactus somersaulted to the floor, Norris Fowler immediately blamed the late-afternoon sun streaming through the classroom window. For weeks, he had been caring for Ms. Penfield's prized collection by following her instructions *exactly*. But as he turned away from the blinding light, the watering can he held knocked over the top-heavy plant.

The one with the orange flower on top.

Her favorite.

He knew it was her favorite, because she had proudly announced to her students that she was planning to enter it at the Blooming Plants Show, one of the many events at next weekend's annual lobster festival.

Down tumbled the cactus, and Norris valiantly tried to grab it, but its vicious spines got in the way and scratched his arms as the plant plunged to the floor. Norris watched in horror as the flower snapped off, shot across the linoleum and came to rest under Ms. Penfield's desk.

Rats, thought Norris.

He scrambled to retrieve the flower, hitting his head on the desk in the process.

"Rats!" he yelped, rubbing the spot where a bump would no doubt appear.

He jumped to his feet, then righted the cactus, placed it back on the shelf and carefully set the flower on top. Slowly, he released his hands.

Quickly, the flower pitched to his feet.

Norris tried again, this time *firmly* pressing

the flower into position. Again, he slowly released his hands.

The flower teetered, then spitefully performed another header to the floor.

"Rats!" shouted Norris. "Rats, rats, rats!!"

Here he was, the envy of his classmates, because Ms. Penfield had finally given him an important assignment, and now look!

How was he supposed to get out of *this* one?

Deep breaths, Norris told himself. First things first.

Norris spun around to see if there were any witnesses. Fortunately, he was quite alone. Only the classroom blackboard stared back at him, full of words from the day's spelling quiz.

Norris, despite the hot water he was in, took a moment to pull out his test from his pocket. His score, 16 out of 20, was underlined in red pen alongside a hand-drawn happy face. It was his best mark, ever! And he was a really lousy speller.

The *worst*, in fact.

Of course, it helped that Norris had cheated off Ferguson. And Norris might have received a perfect score if Ferguson had not caught him and spent the rest of the quiz crouched over his own work in a giant huff. Ferguson, an expert speller, regularly scored 20 out of 20.

Norris neatly refolded his test and tucked it back into his pocket for safe keeping. The cactus flower remained at his feet, its color as bright as icing sugar. At that thought, he smelled his fingertips: they still smelled sweet.

During lunchtime, he had scored a seat beside Georgia and had taken a swipe at the thickly frosted cupcake she had refused to let him try, not even one little bite!

Georgia brought the most delicious lunches to school: cream cheese and cucumber sandwiches, julienne vegetables with special dips, homemade puddings. She always made a big deal of carefully spreading a cloth napkin on her lap, and Norris liked the way she ate with her mouth closed, something most of his classmates did not bother to do.

Norris scooped up the orange flower along with the rest of the cactus, dumped both parts into the classroom's compost bin, then stirred everything inside to bury the evidence. He worried about how long it would take for the prickly disaster to break down into ordinary untraceable soil.

Graeme, of course, would know the answer to that one.

Graeme was another classmate who bugged Norris. He was Mr. Science, always with his head in a book or that boring marine aquarium magazine of his, even at recess. It was ridiculous. Worst of all, Graeme was clearly Ms. Penfield's favorite student, so it came as a staggering surprise to everyone when she chose Norris to take care of her plants while she was off having her baby.

Norris stacked the empty flowerpot inside the other empty ones and assessed the shelf where her prized collection was displayed. The missing cactus left an ugly gap that no amount of rearranging would hide. Plus, the scratch marks on his arms were now bleeding — more evidence that something had gone hideously wrong.

What he needed was a plan, and in his experience, the more cunning the better. Norris made a quick dash for the exit. He did his best thinking on the school's swings, so that was where he headed.

The hilltop playground was awash with children in the after-school program. Their shouts and laughter rose above the *putta-putta* sounds of lobster boats returning in beeline formation to Lower Narrow Spit's government wharf, located across the road below the school.

Norris swooped onto a recently abandoned swing that was still swaying from the last occupant.

"Hey!" shouted some children standing bunched in line, patiently waiting their turn.

"Didn't see you," Norris replied, madly pumping his legs in the air.

Norris thought lineups were a complete waste of time. Besides, as far as he could tell, everyone else in the playground was just horsing around, whereas *he* had a serious problem to solve.

Higher and higher Norris soared, until he gained a spectacular view of the entire harbor. Down below, and running right past the school, was Main Street, along which stood Lower Narrow Spit's commercial buildings: the old dance hall, the curling rink, the bank, the drugstore, the post office, the hardware store, the minimart, the community museum and the diner that sold famous Chinese take-out with special lobster sauce.

Closer to the school, the government wharf perched at the harbor's edge, and beside that stood the town's only lobster cannery.

The cannery, called Lucky Catch, was the most impressive building in the community, an imposing aluminum-clad box with few windows and a gigantic parking lot. Norris spotted his dad's car right away, a powder-blue convertible with red leather seats. It was the only sports car among the rows of mostly pickup trucks.

Norris's dad, Edward Fowler, was the cannery's owner.

"There are three types of people in this world," his dad often reminded Norris. "Those who *work* at the cannery. Those who *buy* from the cannery. And those who *own* the cannery. Which type do you want to be?"

Norris always gave the right answer.

"An owner," he dutifully replied.

"Get off, Norris! It's my turn!" Allen complained.

Allen was a high-pitched grade two student who broke away from the riotous lineup to confront Norris. He was practically hopping as Norris sailed forward and backward over his head.

"In a minute," Norris promised with absolutely no intention of getting off.

Not until he figured out what to do about the missing orange-flowered cactus.

List of Suspects

"I'm telling!" howled Allen as Norris continued to soar just beyond Allen's reach.

Allen spun around in search of someone older to tell.

Norris clucked his tongue and continued to pump unabated, his city-bought sneakers rocketing higher and higher.

"Norris! Stop hogging the swings!" Deckland demanded as he stomped across the playground with Allen in tow.

Deckland was in Norris's grade, and it was his turn to serve as playground monitor. Allen stood slightly behind him with his chicken-thin arms crossed smugly against his chest.

"I said *in a minute*," Norris yelled back, pumping all the more.

How was he supposed to think with all these interruptions?

"Come on, Allen," said Deckland haughtily. "The teeter-totter is free. I'll spot you."

"Some people's kids," muttered Norris as the two marched off.

Norris sliced through the air, his arms straining at the swing's chains on the up climb. The scratch marks on his arms had stopped bleeding, but still. He did not like the thought of disappointing Ms. Penfield.

Norris recalled all those classroom faces of disbelief when she had assigned him the coveted task. Now those same faces would wear looks that read, "We *told* you Norris couldn't be trusted."

Which was absolutely not fair. The class *still*

blamed Norris for the incident way back in grade two when he had flooded the boys' bathroom. He had been demonstrating how fun it was to shove unusual things down the toilet — marbles, a lost-and-found sock, felt markers that turned the swirling water into rainbows — and everyone had cheered him on until water overflowed, then spilled past the cubicle, into the hall and under the door of the teachers' lunchroom.

The whole class got detention.

And no one would let him forget it.

Well, Norris had a good memory, too. And there were plenty at school who had done *him* wrong. He kept a running tally.

Wait! That was it!

Norris stopped pumping.

He could finally put his list of annoying students to good use!

Norris would write down the names of suspects who might want to get him in trouble by *stealing* the cactus. Then he would get someone to investigate, and at the same time shed enough suspicion that everyone would be blamed.

And Norris would get off the hook!

Norris jumped from the swings. The bunched-up line of children cheered at the vacant seat while he sprinted down the schoolyard hill and back into his homeroom. He grabbed a sheet of paper from his desk and sat down to compose his list.

Norris's pencil paused in the air. There were so many offenders to choose from. He decided that he would focus on the most recent ones. Norris wrote their names in bold letters as he thought about their wrongdoings:

Alin (*That tattletale!* thought Norris.)
Deklan (*The big hero!*)
Gorgia (*For refusing to share her lunch!*)
Ferguson (*Who hid his test!*)

That's plenty, thought Norris.

Now all he needed to do was figure out who would conduct the investigation. It would have to be someone who would take the work seriously, someone who was trustworthy, someone who would get the job done *before* Ms. Penfield came to pick up her missing cactus for the lobster festival.

Norris studied the room for clues, but someone outside the window caught his attention. It was Ferguson standing in a grove of trees right beside the school, hands clasped, staring pensively at the ground.

Ferguson was hard to miss. He wore the same kind of sweater vests as the old fishermen who lived at Sunset Manor, the local seniors' residence. And besides winning spelling bees, Ferguson would pose the oddest questions.

"How can we agree about things that aren't real?" he once asked Ms. Penfield during recess.

"Pardon me?" Ms. Penfield had replied.

"Well, how can we agree to rules about a game like dodgeball when rules are just made up?"

Dodgeball was Norris's favorite sport. He could actually sense which way players planned to duck, then strike with remarkable aim.

But Ferguson hated the game, complaining bitterly whenever he was hit, which was a lot, because he was such a slow mover.

And anytime a classroom pet died — a hamster, a tree frog, a garden snake — it was Ferguson who insisted on serving as funeral director, making sure that everything got a proper burial at the little cemetery he had staked out in the grove. He was probably burying something now.

Norris continued to search the room for clues as to who should conduct his investigation. He spotted a hand-written sign above the classroom's goldfish bowl that read "Do not overfeed."

It was Graeme's writing. Mr. Scientific Principles. Mr. Rules of Deduction. Mr. Problem Solver.

Graeme would be perfect!

There was still the question about the scratch marks on Norris's arms. How was he going to explain them away?

Norris smiled. In a flash of brilliance, he saw how he could bamboozle Graeme about his arms and get him to agree to Norris's investigation in one fell swoop.

But first, Norris needed a box.

Fortunately, he knew exactly where to get one.

Norris arrived at the cannery by taking a shortcut through the now almost-empty parking lot. He paused as he passed by his dad's convertible.

The dent on the passenger door was still there.

Norris's ears went pink.

A month ago, just before Ms. Penfield left to

have her baby, Norris had been practicing his aim for dodgeball in the courtyard beside the school. He had been repeatedly throwing the ball against the brick wall and catching it as it flew back to him, irritated that gym class had ended before he could be declared dodgeball winner.

"Hello, son," his dad had called to Norris as he climbed out of his car. "I'm here to meet Ms. Penfield. It's parent-teacher interviews today."

Norris, who was not a big fan of these meetings because he never *ever* received the stellar reports that he felt he deserved, wanted to show off his exceptional dodgeball skills.

"Catch!" he replied, and he bounced the ball to his dad.

To Norris's dismay, the ball ricocheted off a bump in the pavement, completely missed his dad and careened into the side of the unfortunately parked car.

Norris's dad stood there in his suit and pastel-dotted tie, angrily jingling coins in his pocket as he assessed the damage.

Norris braced himself.

"Norris," his dad lectured. "There are three types of people in this world. Those who *make* dodgeballs. Those who *play* with dodgeballs. And those who *own* the dodgeball factory. Which type do you want to be?"

Norris scuffed at the ground.

"An owner," he muttered.

Norris's dad adjusted his tie.

"Then put that ball away and wait for me in the car."

His dad strode into the school without a backward glance.

Norris picked up the dodgeball and turned back to the brick wall where he had been doing so well only moments before. Then he spotted

Ms. Penfield at an open window, looking down at him in the courtyard.

Had she heard the whole sorry exchange?

Norris could not be sure, but the very next day she had assigned him to take care of her plants.

Norris shook his head at the memory. He proceeded past the dented car to the cannery and walked by his dad's office window. His dad was inside, sitting at his executive desk, absorbed in some report he was reading and underlining things with his fancy fountain pen. He did not see Norris slip past his window and through the front doors.

Lucky Catch

Norris headed straight down the hall to where he knew the cannery supplies were kept. He stepped inside the storage room, which was filled with tin cans, packaging labels and empty boxes. Everything was plastered with the Lucky Catch logo: a cartoon lobster rowing a dory with its giant claws, its tail tipped up in the air as if waving.

Norris tossed through an assortment of boxes in order to find the perfect size for his purposes: not too big and not too small.

There! That one!

He grabbed the box and headed back down the hall.

"Hello, Norris," said a cannery worker, one of Ferguson's many sisters, but whose name he could not recall.

She wore a hairnet and an apron stamped with the Lucky Catch logo, and was headed to the factory part of the cannery, where the lobsters were cracked open after being boiled.

He gave her a curt nod as he sailed by with his box.

No one ever questioned Norris at the cannery; he could take whatever he wanted.

Once outside, Norris hustled the box up Main Street to Deckland's house, knowing that Deckland was still monitoring the playground. He easily spotted Deckland's black-and-white kitten, which was prowling around an enormous whale bone that Deckland's family displayed in their front flower garden.

Deckland had been bragging to Norris about the new kitten for days, which annoyed Norris to no end. Norris was not allowed pets. His family traveled far too much to bother with kennels and the like, no matter how much Norris begged.

"Come here, little kitten," said Norris, using his gentlest voice.

He crouched down and patiently held out his hand. The kitten came to inspect. Norris scratched her silky head, then gently scooped the kitten to his chest to rub her skinny back. The warm kitten began to purr.

"Okay, little kitten," said Norris. "I'm going to put you in this cozy box so that we can go on a short walk. But don't worry. You'll be back home in a jiffy."

Norris eased the kitten into the box and closed the lid. He slowly picked up the container so as not to tip out the contents. Then he turned and headed to the home of his soon-to-be investigator, Mr. Science.

Graeme's house, which also stood on Main Street, looked okay from a distance. But as Norris drew closer, he could see that the house needed a good paint job. A few roof shingles were missing, too, and the lilac bush blocking part of the front porch needed pruning. All in all, Norris concluded, the house was typical for a lobster fisherman.

As Norris got closer still, he spotted Fetch, Graeme's old beagle, sprawled out at the top of the steps, tongue sprawled out, too.

"Aren't you the good guard dog," Norris teased when he got to the top of the steps.

Fetch thumped his tail once, but otherwise did not move.

Norris stepped over Fetch, carefully juggled the box to one hip and rapped as loudly as he could on the screen door.

"Graeme!" Norris called. "You home?"

"Hi, Norris," said Graeme flatly, coming to the door and talking through the screen, arms crossed. "I was just leaving to meet my dad."

Graeme spoke in that infuriating know-it-all tone he often used in class whenever he answered a question that Norris could not. Graeme had a knack for making Norris feel like a complete idiot.

But Norris was on a mission, so he ignored Graeme's rudeness.

"Know what I've got?" asked Norris pleasantly.

Graeme looked him up and down as if Norris was a specimen in one of his science projects.

Norris noticed that Graeme paused when he eyed the Big Fish Aquarium ball cap that Norris was wearing, a souvenir from his family's last vacation. Norris knew for a fact that Graeme had never been very far from Lower Narrow Spit.

Graeme grudgingly pushed open the screen door and stepped onto the porch, taking care not to disturb Fetch.

Norris set down the box and opened the lid. He reached inside and lifted out the puny kitten. She wiggled and struggled about with pitiful mews, while Norris deliberately held her away from him in an attempt to fool Graeme into thinking that Norris did not know how to handle small pets.

"No wonder you're scratched up. You're holding her all wrong," observed Graeme. "Here. Let me."

Norris handed the flailing kitten to Graeme, careful not to smile at Graeme's arrogance.

Graeme nestled the kitten into his chest and stroked her back, just as Norris had done earlier on Deckland's front lawn. The kitten immediately burrowed into Graeme's T-shirt and began to purr.

Norris watched, arms covered in scratch marks made by the cactus, not the kitten.

"Would you look at that!" said Norris, pretending to be impressed, all according to plan. Then, without missing a beat, he added, "Think you could help me solve an even bigger problem?"

Graeme took ages to answer Norris's simple request.

"Depends," he finally replied.

Norris could see that Graeme was only half listening, because the kitten was now licking his neck with her pink sandpaper tongue.

"I'm in big trouble," said Norris, pressing on. "One of Ms. Penfield's cacti is missing."

Norris was careful not to say "cactuses," having been publicly humiliated by Graeme about the correct plural for cactus a dozen times.

Graeme looked up.

"Missing?" Graeme repeated. "Which one?"

There. That condescending tone again.

"The one with the orange flower on top," Norris confessed, shoving his annoyance at Graeme's attitude back down. "I was on the swings after school today, and then I remembered I had to water the plants. So I came back in, only the cactus wasn't there anymore."

Which was true. Norris had just left out the accident part, which would explain the plant's mysterious disappearance.

"Ms. Penfield told me that one took *years* to flower," Graeme remarked. He leaned on the word "years."

Norris did not detect even a smidgen of sympathy.

"All I know is that she was planning on entering it at the lobster festival's plant show," lamented Norris. "And now it's gone!"

"Well, there's got to be a logical explanation," Graeme said authoritatively while rubbing the kitten against his cheek.

Graeme was playing right into Norris's hands. Norris knew that Graeme prided himself on applying scientific rules and deductions every chance he got. That's why everyone was convinced he was so smart.

But Norris also knew that not everything could be explained by logic. The hatching of an ingenious plan, for example, was much more art than science.

"You know what I think," said Norris. It was time to lower the trap. "I think someone has *stolen* that cactus. Someone who doesn't like me."

Norris paused for dramatic effect, then dug into his pocket and produced a folded piece of paper. He handed it to Graeme.

"Here's my list of suspects."

Accused

Graeme scanned Norris's list, which the kitten
tried to bat away.

"Why isn't Lynnette on your list?" he asked.

Lynnette was Graeme's rambunctious little
sister. Ever since she had won the pageant title
of Princess Mermaid during last year's annual
lobster festival, she had ordered everyone around
as if they were her royal subjects.

Norris admired her spunk, which he showed
by pulling her hat over her eyes whenever he
crossed her path.

"Lynnette doesn't like me?" he asked in bewilderment.

"Not even a little," said Graeme.

"What's *her* problem?" asked Norris, genuinely hurt by Graeme's cruel words.

"You keep pulling her hat down over her eyes whenever you walk by."

"You do that, too!"

"I'm her brother."

"Oh," said Norris, not really understanding the difference, but also not wanting to be further lectured by the likes of Graeme.

"So are you going to help me, or what?" asked Norris, more crankily than he intended.

"No," said Graeme, returning the list to Norris.

Norris could feel his ears burn pink. He had been so sure that his plan to enlist Graeme was foolproof.

"Fine," Norris said with tight lips. "It's no skin off my nose."

He snatched the kitten from Graeme and stuffed her back in the box. At the same moment, there were shouts and cheers down at the government wharf.

Both boys rushed to look from the porch railing. An unusually large crowd had gathered by Graeme's dad's lobster boat, *Homarus II*, which had returned home for the day and was tied to the wharf along with the rest of the fleet.

"I wonder what's rattling their socks?" Norris said. It was something his dad often asked while he observed the lobster fishermen on the wharf from his cannery office window.

"I better get going," Graeme said, clearly happy for an excuse to leave.

"Yeah, well, I've got things to do, too," said Norris, bending down to pick up his box.

By the time he stood again, Graeme had given him the slip.

Rats, thought Norris, holding a useless box housing a useless kitten. Still, he refused to give up. He knew that if he did, his dad would no doubt hear about Norris's failure with the cactus.

Norris could already hear the three-types-of-people lecture: those who *worked* at the plant store, those who *bought* from the plant store and those who *owned* the plant store, so which type did Norris want to be?

Not the type who lives on Main Street, Norris thought as he trudged toward Deckland's house with his box.

Deckland's whale bone was not the only tacky garden item on display in Lower Narrow Spit. Norris could also make out Georgia's house with its collection of plastic lawn chairs under a screened-in bug tent; Allen's house with its primitive folk-art bird feeders; and Ferguson's house surrounded by a trampled yard choked with outdoor sporting equipment, including a badminton net, horseshoes and lawn darts.

Norris took comfort that his own house with its fancy gingerbread trim on all four sides, not just the front, was far from the gaudiness of Main Street. His family owned a point of land called Marshy Hope, which was on the outskirts of Lower Narrow Spit. His dad had bought the land from an old fisherman named McDermit, who had kept his fish shed and lobster traps on it.

McDermit's shed had been bulldozed long ago to make way for the Fowler family's tennis court. The only thing that remained was the shed's handmade door handle, which Norris's mom had found so quaint that she had framed it and hung it in their new home's kitchen pantry.

The kitten started scratching from inside the box as Norris crossed Deckland's front yard.

He opened the box and carefully lifted out the tiny pet. She immediately spotted a butterfly and playfully pounced after it.

"What do you think you're doing?!" demanded Deckland, who stormed from around the corner of his house and in his haste let the garage door swing wide open.

Deckland was holding a wet paintbrush in his hand. Norris guessed that he had been working on his family's float for the upcoming lobster festival parade, having finished his shift as playground monitor.

Deckland's family ran a hardware store called the Toolbox, and they participated in the parade to advertise the tools that they sold.

"Nothing!" Norris insisted, while hiding the empty box behind his back.

Deckland eyed Norris suspiciously.

"It's never *nothing* with you," Deckland accused, pointing his dripping paintbrush at Norris and coming dangerously close to his polo shirt.

Norris took a hasty step back. His mom would absolutely kill him if he came home with a paint stain on his expensive clothes.

"You can't be trusted," Deckland said, taking a menacing step to close the gap.

"That was a long time ago!" complained Norris, for he was certain that Deckland was referring to the incident when they had been playing in Deckland's garage some months after the toilet-flooding affair.

Norris had convinced him to open all the leftover cans of paint. One thing had led to another, and the boys had somehow ended up painting Deckland's family van, which to this day Norris defends, because the van was old and rusty.

Not like his dad's powder-blue convertible with the red leather seats.

Dent aside.

The kitten rubbed up against Deckland's leg.

"Come here, Nails," he cooed as he tossed his brush to the grass and scooped up the kitten.

"Nails?" Norris repeated. "I suppose that name makes sense if your family is into hardware."

"We can't all own Lower Narrow Spit's only lobster cannery, if that's what you're getting at," Deckland snapped. There was poison in his voice.

"There's no need to get huffy," Norris said. He had been trying to be nice about the kitten's name and not at all rubbing it in that canneries trump hardware stores any day. "Some people's kids," he muttered as he strode away.

Norris had no time for the likes of Deckland and his ridiculously named kitten. But when he got closer to the cannery to return the empty box, his mood further soured. Once again, he was faced with the problem of Ms. Penfield's missing cactus.

Deadly Aim

Norris took a deep breath, then peeked in the window of his dad's office. He was surprised to see that his dad was no longer alone. On the opposite side of his monstrous desk sat Georgia and her dad. Georgia's family owned Tasty Foods, the town's minimart, and about this time every year, they came in to place an extra-large order of lobster for the upcoming festival.

Norris ducked past the window and into the cannery. He crept stealthily down the hall and stopped short of the office door so that he could eavesdrop.

Eavesdropping was his next-favorite activity, right after dodgeball.

"So you'll have a word with Norris?" asked Georgia's dad.

"Of course," said Norris's dad testily. "I have no idea why he would run off with Georgia's lunches when he brings more than enough to eat from home."

Norris nearly dropped the box. That hateful tattletale! How *dare* she?

"Well, Georgia *is* pretty good in the kitchen," said her dad apologetically, as if to smooth out the awkward conversation. "In fact," he added with pride, "Georgia is entering this year's lobster chowder contest."

"I've created my very own recipe," said Georgia, chiming in.

"I've created my very own recipe," Norris mimicked under his breath. "Some people's kids."

"Is that a fact," said Norris's dad.

Norris recognized the cold tone; it was the one his dad often used on his staff when they complained about his "big city ideas."

"Then I look forward to tasting it. I'm this year's judge," Norris's dad informed his visitors.

Georgia's dad pushed his chair back and got up to shake hands.

"Well, no hard feelings then. We best be on our way, right, Georgia?"

More chair scraping.

Norris took his cue and hustled down the hall to hide out in the storage room until the coast was clear. He sat among the supplies and stewed.

No wonder Georgia had made his list of suspects!

And Deckland, for that matter!

But Norris could only fume for so long. Slowly he stood. Even though he still hoped he could worm his way out of taking the blame for Ms. Penfield's cactus, he could not avoid his dad's lecture about Georgia's lunches, having been caught red-handed.

Norris plodded down the hall and slunk into his dad's office as silently as rolling fog. His dad did not see him. He was too busy staring out of his window at the commotion on the government wharf while jingling the coins in his pocket. His suit and tie sharply contrasted with the rubber coveralls worn by the fishermen he was watching.

Norris took a minute to look around. No matter how many visits he paid to his dad's office, Norris was always astounded by the contents. Sure, there were the expected stacks of ledgers and thick binders filled with federal regulations about fishing that were piled on his dad's desk. But the walls were something else. They were decorated with the heads of big-game trophies: a grizzly bear, an Alaska wolf, an antelope, a mule deer, two elk, a bighorn sheep, a bull moose and a buffalo.

It was a smorgasbord of fangs and antlers, and any cannery worker who did not know that it was Norris's legendary *grandfather* who had hunted these animals, and not his dad, would surely be intimidated. Norris's grandfather used to own Lucky Catch, but he had turned it over to his son-in-law once he agreed to leave the city and move with Norris's mom to Lower Narrow Spit when Norris was born.

There was one more object that Norris checked on before he announced his presence. It was the water-filled paperweight that he had made at school for his dad sometime during the toilet-flooding, van-painting era. It featured a tiny toy boat that danced in the waves. Norris had even painted his dad's name on the starboard and port sides of the bow.

Unfortunately, the water had leaked out long ago, so that the boat looked abandoned at low tide. And yet, despite the paperweight's forlorn and out-of-place appearance, Norris's dad had kept it all the same.

Norris cleared his throat.

His dad turned and frowned at the interruption, but his expression changed to surprise when he saw Norris.

"Hello, son," he said, not sounding all that pleased to see him.

Norris hung his head and braced for the lecture about Georgia's lunches.

"Did you see the giant lobster on your way in?" his dad continued in an unexpected turn.

"What giant lobster?" Norris asked, daring to look up.

"The one that Graeme's father, Swinimer, just caught. You can see it on the stern of his boat. That's what's rattling everyone's socks at the wharf."

Norris skirted the desk to get to the window. There was, indeed, a giant lobster hunkering

down on the floorboards of *Homarus II* while
Graeme helped his dad hose off the day's bait
from the boat.

Even from where Norris stood, he could see
Graeme's jubilant smile.

"You don't sound very happy about it," Norris
said.

"That's because Swinimer wouldn't sell it to
me," Norris's dad said, fiercely jingling his coins,
"even when I told him it would make a great
trophy for the cannery."

Norris eyed his grandfather's wall trophies.
Was his dad trying to make the cannery office
more his own?

"What does Graeme's dad want to do with it?"
Norris asked.

"For now, he'll move it into a tank at the
community museum. Then he says he's going
to put it up for auction at the lobster festival,"
Norris's dad explained, not taking his eyes

off the giant catch. "And if the lobster gets the highest bid of the evening, Graeme's dad will win the prize money for donating the best item."

"What's he going to do with the money?" Norris asked as Graeme coiled the hose, then waved good-bye to his dad and the other fishermen, practically skipping down the wharf for home. "Paint his house? Shingle his roof? Hire a gardener?"

"He wants to take Graeme on a trip to Big Fish Aquarium."

Norris recalled how Graeme had enviously stared at Norris's souvenir ball cap.

In an instant, a new and improved plan to cover up the cactus accident unfolded in Norris's mind. Only now, it would involve Graeme *and* his dad's giant catch.

"That lobster would sure make a fine trophy," said Norris with the deadly aim of a champion dodgeball player. "Way better than any of granddad's."

"You know what I think," said Norris's dad. It was not a question. "*I'm* going to be the highest bidder at that auction, come hell or high water. Then everyone in Lower Narrow Spit will know, once and for all, who's who around here."

He turned back to the window, staring hard at the scene on the wharf behind the glass, coins a-jiggling.

Norris smiled. He edged his way to the door, having just set his cunning scheme into motion. He almost made it.

"By the way, Norris," said his dad without turning away from the window.

Norris froze.

"What's wrong with your lunches?"

"Nothing," said Norris, scuffing at the floor.

"Good," said Norris's dad. "Then I trust you'll leave everyone else's food alone."

"Yes," said Norris.

"Even homemade cupcakes," said Norris's dad.

"Yes," squeaked Norris.

"With orange icing," pressed Norris's dad relentlessly.

"Yes," whispered Norris, ears pink, fingers still sticky.

Marshy Hope

Norris dashed out of the cannery, scooted across the parking lot, then headed straight up Main Street to Graeme's house. Even from a distance, he could spot Graeme standing at his porch railing, overlooking the harbor below. Graeme appeared lost in thought and did not see him coming.

"Norris!" someone else shouted.

Norris turned.

Rats.

It was Ferguson, angrily charging toward him.

Even if Norris had wanted to hide, there were no bushes or other concealments nearby. So he stood his ground.

"What's up?" he asked innocently.

Ferguson marched to within a hair's breadth of Norris.

Norris might have been more nervous, if not for the fact that Ferguson was rather comically carting a bat-shaped kite over the shoulder of his sweater vest.

"You know what's up! You're one gigantic cheater!" accused Ferguson, shifting the kite to his other shoulder. "I could just spit feathers!"

"Try not to go overboard," said Norris, dismissively. But then he suddenly recalled Ferguson's argument against dodgeball. "Who cares about spelling, anyway? As far as I can tell, the rules are just made up. It's all pretend, if you ask me."

Ferguson practically staggered backward.

"Words are not *pretend*," he countered. "In fact, they're more real than people, if you think about it."

Norris stood baffled.

"What?" he asked, scratching the bump on his head.

"Words are more real than people," Ferguson repeated with conviction.

Norris gave Ferguson his blankest stare.

"People die, but words go on and on and on. They're *eternal*," said Ferguson. "That makes them more real than you or me."

It was just like Ferguson to jam one of his dark philosophical observations into an otherwise ordinary conversation.

"You're creeping me out," admitted Norris, determined to lighten the mood. "What's with the bat kite?"

"I'm going to fly it with my granddad. He lives at Sunset Manor."

"Sunset Manor? Where all the old fishermen live?"

"Senior citizens," Ferguson corrected.

"Must be a dull place," said Norris. "I hear they just sit around making gawd-awful crafts for the lobster festival. Graeme won a lamp made of lobster cans last year. It was hideous."

"They do more than crafts!" Ferguson argued. "There's ping-pong and cards and lawn bowling and museum outings and" — he lifted the bat — "kite flying."

Norris remained unimpressed. But then he remembered something about one of the residents at Sunset Manor.

"Say," Norris said. "My dad bought our land at Marshy Hope from an old fisherman named McDermit. I'm pretty sure he moved to Sunset Manor."

"He's not at Sunset Manor anymore," Ferguson said, his angry tone now replaced with sorrow. "He died a year ago. My granddad still misses him."

Norris recalled the homemade door handle from McDermit's shed, now framed and hanging in his mom's pantry. Would Ferguson think that door handles are more real than people, too?

He decided not to ask.

There were more cheers down at the wharf, and both boys turned to look.

"Have you seen the giant lobster?" Norris asked, pleased to be the first to share the latest gossip.

"What giant lobster?" Ferguson replied.

"Graeme's dad caught it," Norris explained.

"McDermit caught a giant lobster back in the day," Ferguson said. "He once showed me a newspaper article about it in his scrapbook."

"The one just caught is still at the wharf, if you want to go see it," said Norris.

He was eager for Ferguson to leave so he could make his way back to Graeme's house, all part of his new plan.

Ferguson licked his pointer finger and held it high to test the wind.

"I can't. The wind's going to die soon," he concluded.

"They'll be moving the lobster to the community museum for now," Norris offered. "You could go ask your grandfather if he wants to check it out later this week."

"That's not a bad idea," said Ferguson.

With that he turned and headed down Main Street, bat kite fluttering against his back.

Ferguson dispensed with, Norris quickly set his sights on Graeme's house. Graeme was still on the porch. Perfect!

Norris raced along the street, then up the stairs, taking two steps at a time, waving vigorously at Graeme as he climbed.

Graeme responded by ducking behind the overgrown lilac bush, pretending to have spotted an unusual insect, or something.

"I heard the news!" Norris puffed as he scrambled up the last of the steps. "That's one huge lobster!"

Norris stood on the porch to catch his breath, strategically adjusting his Big Fish ball cap.

Graeme jealously eyed the cap, just as Norris knew he would.

"My dad's going to auction it off at this year's lobster festival," Graeme boasted. "Then *we'll* be going to Big Fish. Well, that is, if it brings in the highest bid of the evening."

Norris detected uncertainty in Graeme's voice. It was all he could do not to rub his hands in glee.

"You know what I think," Norris said. "No one's going to bid on that giant lobster. The meat will be too tough to eat, if you ask me."

"Tough, maybe," Graeme agreed, smug tone taking hold. "But some people might want it for a trophy. Take your dad, for instance."

"That's what I thought," Norris said. "But I just talked to my dad at the cannery, and he's only lukewarm about the idea."

"Didn't seem lukewarm down at the wharf," Graeme argued.

"Oh, he's lukewarm all right," Norris announced with authority.

Even now, Norris was not fibbing. He had spent countless hours watching his dad at the cannery. While his dad's reaction to the giant lobster was intense, it was *nothing* compared to his ongoing frustration over broken cannery equipment, which he suspected his employees had something to do with.

Graeme grasped the railing of the porch and looked out over the empty bay.

Norris allowed Graeme to despair for a couple of minutes. Then he cast Graeme a life ring.

"You know what I think. I can talk my dad into bidding really high on your dad's giant lobster."

Graeme sighed.

"What's the catch?"

Norris dug into his pocket and produced his list of suspects once again.

"Help me solve the cactus mystery," Norris said, fluttering the list in front of Graeme's face like bait.

"Deal," said Graeme, snatching the paper from Norris.

Norris beamed and headed down the stairs for home. There was no turning the tide back now. Graeme's investigation was a go.

Decoy

Norris sat at his school desk, trying very hard not to look at the gap in the plant collection by the window of their classroom. Nobody had noticed the missing cactus yet, but Norris knew that it was only a matter of time.

Had Graeme begun his investigation? Norris could not be sure. He looked over at Graeme, who had been thrusting his hand up relentlessly in response to every single question that their fill-in teacher asked. He had his hand up now.

Norris rolled his eyes. Then he looked over at Georgia. She somehow felt his gaze and turned to scowl at him. Today, she had brought a towering slice of banana cream pie in her lunch, and Norris had not been able to resist.

Norris turned away from her hostile glower and locked eyes with Deckland. Deckland was even less friendly, having earlier accused Norris of not properly cleaning his paintbrush during that morning's art class. Deckland was particular about the brushes, which the Toolbox had donated to the school just that week.

Norris tapped Ferguson on the shoulder. Ferguson merely shrugged him off, then protectively hunkered over his schoolwork, as if Norris was trying to copy an answer.

Some people's kids, Norris concluded with disgust.

Adrift in the classroom, Norris's thoughts turned to last night's supper, which his dad had made because Norris's mom had to meet with the volunteer steering committee for the lobster festival. The meal had started off as a gloomy affair. The cannery's boiler had been acting up again, making it difficult for staff to fill the minimart's extra-large order.

"You wouldn't believe how grumpy everyone is about working overtime," his dad had complained as he speared the peas on his plate. "You'd think they'd be happy with all the bonus pay!"

To cheer his dad up, Norris had presented his spelling test, 16 out of 20, with the penned happy face.

"Terrific," said Norris's dad. "I'll post it on my office door to show everyone that the next cannery owner is following in his dad's footsteps."

Norris had beamed with pride.

The afternoon recess bell rang, and Norris charged out the door, straight to the playground swings, to get his mind off his troubles. It worked, but not in the way Norris wanted. Allen spent the entire time yelling that it was his turn and beseeching anyone who would listen to help him kick Norris off.

Still, by the end of the school day, no one had said anything about Ms. Penfield's plant, much to Norris's relief. Then, after stopping by the cannery to make sure that his dad *had* posted his test, Norris made his way to Graeme's house for an update on the investigation.

Graeme was not home yet, so Norris stood at the railing, patted Fetch and waited. He also picked at the new scab forming on his elbow, caused when he had slipped on the linoleum as he tried to run off with Georgia's slice of pie.

Eventually, Norris spotted Graeme walking home from the direction of the community museum. He remembered that Graeme had been tasked with feeding the giant lobster until the auction.

"Hi, Graeme," said Norris as Graeme climbed the last of the stairs. "I'm here for my status report."

Norris repositioned his Big Fish ball cap, a move designed to keep up the pressure.

"I've just eliminated one suspect," said Graeme, bending down to scratch Fetch after eyeing Norris's souvenir.

"Who?" asked Norris.

"Allen Carrington."

"Allen was a long shot," said Norris. He began to snap his fingers, which was his pet signal to get on with it. "You better get cracking on that list. The festival is only a week away. Tasty Foods has already placed their extra-large order at the cannery for frozen lobster."

"Don't worry about your list," said Graeme peevishly. "I'll get through it in time."

"You know what I think," said Norris. "You're worried."

He sat down on the porch rocker and began to creak back and forth.

Creak, creak. Creak, creak.

Fetch raised his eyebrows at the unpleasant noise, but otherwise did not move.

"Watch Fetch's tail," warned Graeme. "Your rocker's getting awfully close."

"I'm nowhere near Fetch's tail," argued Norris, but he scooted his rocker back just the same. "I'm good with animals, you know."

"I bet," Graeme taunted. "Say, how's your kitten?"

Norris was confused.

"What kitten?" he asked.

He stopped creaking.

"*What kitten?*" Graeme repeated incredulously. "The one you brought over yesterday!"

Norris stared blankly at him.

"In a *cannery box*," Graeme said as if speaking to an imbecile.

It dawned on Norris that Graeme was talking about Deckland's kitten, which Norris had used as a decoy in his first attempt to dupe Graeme.

"Oh," said Norris. "*That* kitten."

Creak, creak. Creak, creak.

Norris noticed Graeme studying Norris's arms. The scratch marks from the cactus were healing nicely compared to the fresh scrape caused by Georgia's pie.

"At least you're holding her better."

Norris shrugged. If he kept quiet, Graeme was bound to jump to his own wrong conclusion.

Graeme shot Norris a suspicious look.

"Did something happen to the kitten?" Graeme asked.

"What? No! The kitten's fine," Norris said, returning his attention to his scabby elbow.

"You're sure?" Graeme persisted.

Norris stopped picking. Graeme was like a dog gnawing a bone!

"Sure, I'm sure. Look, I think we should review my list of suspects," he said.

"Okay. By the way, you never told me your kitten's name," said Graeme.

"My kitten's name?" Norris repeated in an attempt to stall.

"Yes, your kitten's name," said Graeme. "Stop stalling."

Creak, creak. Creak, creak.

Graeme kept staring through narrowed eyes. At last, Norris relented.

"The kitten's name is Nails," he said, knowing that his answer was going to sound stupid because his family did not own a hardware store.

"*Nails?* " Graeme said with predictable sarcasm. "You named your kitten *Nails?* Kittens have claws, Norris. *People* have nails."

"Well, I didn't name her," Norris snapped, which was true. "And enough about the kitten. Let's get to your suspect list, because you're running out of time, if you ask me."

"*Nails!*" Graeme repeated, still scoffing as if Norris had only one oar in the water. He pulled the list out of his pocket and scanned it.

"Who's next?" demanded Norris, having another go at his scab.

Double-Cross

When Norris lumbered down the stairs to
the quiet kitchen of his empty house the next
morning, a note on the refrigerator told him why
there was no one home. His mom had gone to the
city for her hair appointment, and the boiler was
still acting up at the cannery.

Norris wandered into the kitchen. Sure
enough, a bowl of cereal, a banana and a muffin
were set out neatly on the table before him.

Norris picked up the muffin.

It was bran.

Rats, thought Norris.

He went to the refrigerator in search of leftover chocolate cake, but then remembered that he had scarfed down the last piece the night before. He returned to his seat and glumly ate his meal near the pantry displaying McDermit's framed door handle.

Breakfast done, the whole Saturday yawned and stretched before him. And, as happened every single weekend, he sighed at having nothing to do.

But wait! What about the giant lobster? Perhaps he should go visit the community museum and check it out. He might even run into Graeme, which would give him a chance to keep up the pressure. Norris hurriedly got dressed, then bolted outdoors, waving to the gardener who was working the ride-on lawnmower.

The community museum was a hike from Marshy Hope, so by the time Norris entered the building, a former train station, he was sticky and tired. He easily spotted the tank housing the prized lobster and plunked down on a nearby bench to catch his breath.

A small crowd had gathered around the tank. The giant lobster stared at them with its beady eyes, but otherwise did not move.

What a boring giant lobster, thought Norris.

Voices drifted over to where he sat. Norris turned his head to listen better.

It was Ms. Carrington, the museum's director, and Graeme, talking in her office.

Norris perked up.

He stood and carefully sneaked toward her office door, past a rope-framed plaster-of-paris plaque embedded with lobster claws. Even in Norris's sleuthing mode, he stopped to observe how amateurishly made the plaque was in comparison to the professionally framed fish shed door handle that his family had at home.

Norris moved on, then pressed himself against the wall, as close to Ms. Carrington's office door as he dared. The voices were quite clear now.

"That's *our* government wharf!" Graeme was saying.

Norris took a quick peek. Graeme and Ms. Carrington were studying a newspaper article in an old scrapbook on her desk.

"Very observant!" said Ms. Carrington. "The fisherman's name was McDermit. He passed away last year, I think."

Norris pulled back to mull this over. McDermit had once caught a giant lobster. Ferguson said so. That must be what the article was about.

"It doesn't say what happened to the lobster," said Graeme.

"No, it doesn't. But I don't think it ended up as a trophy. The McDermit family donated a number of interesting items to the museum, like this scrapbook, for instance, but a giant mounted lobster wasn't one of them," said Ms. Carrington.

Norris eased away from the door and returned

to the cannery exhibit to ponder this news. Would Graeme think his dad's giant lobster was highly valuable because there was no other trophy like it around? If so, he might decide that he did not need Norris's help, that there would be plenty of bidders from all over at the auction!

Norris looked up to see Ms. Carrington leave her office with the article in her hand. He followed her to the photocopier.

"Hello, Ms. Carrington," said Norris, using his best manners. "What do you have there?"

"I'm helping Graeme with an investigation," she said as she made a copy of the article. "He wants to find out what happened to a giant lobster that a fisherman named McDermit caught."

"But McDermit's dead, right?" said Norris. "So how's Graeme going to find out?"

"Graeme's very clever," Ms. Carrington declared. "He's going to ask McDermit's friends at Sunset Manor." She pointed to two boats tied to the wharf in the article's photograph. Their names were painted on the sterns.

"*Crack of Dawn* and *Fog Burner*," she announced. "Graeme's going to track down the owners."

Norris fumed. Graeme *was* trying to outsmart him by conducting a side investigation of his own, to prove that there was nothing in Lower Narrow Spit like his dad's giant lobster! Well, Norris would have to scuttle that plan!

"Graeme's in my office," said Ms. Carrington, clearly unaware of Graeme's double-crossing intentions. "Do you want to say hi?"

If Norris was going to best Graeme, he could not let Graeme know that he was on to Graeme's diabolical scheme.

"Another time," said Norris, barely containing his outrage.

He made a quick dash for the exit while

Ms. Carrington returned to her office to give Graeme his copy of the article.

Norris spent the rest of the weekend consumed with thoughts about Graeme's planned sabotage at Sunset Manor. Running into Ferguson on Main Street was his only break from brooding. This time, Ferguson was carting an old canvas-covered life ring.

"What's with the life ring?" Norris asked.

Ferguson held the preserver up for better viewing. The name *Fog Burner* was painted on it.

"This was my granddad's," Ferguson explained. "He hung it in my bedroom when he retired."

"Your grandfather owned a boat named *Fog Burner?*" Norris asked, instantly making the connection to the old newspaper photograph in Ms. Carrington's office.

"Nothing gets past you," Ferguson said dryly.

"Where are you going with it?" Norris asked.

"My granddad wants to display it at the Know the Ropes Show."

"What's the Know the Ropes Show?" Norris asked.

"We're going to organize Sunset Manor's own museum exhibit, as part of the lobster festival. Everyone will put something in, mostly old fishing gear and boat stuff, and then sit around and talk about lost trophies."

"Lost trophies?" Norris repeated, picturing his dad's office stuffed with hunting prizes.

"You know. A million fishing stories that all end in 'the one that got away,' " explained Ferguson with a note of affection.

Norris had a panicky thought. If the retired fishermen were lacking trophies, was it likely they would let the giant lobster go to an outside bidder?

Not likely, he quickly realized. But if he could infiltrate Sunset Manor, he might figure out how to squelch Graeme's plan to drive up the bidding, leaving Norris's dad as the only real bidder whom Graeme could depend on.

"Can I come?" Norris asked.

"No," Ferguson said without any hesitation.

"Why not?" asked Norris.

"My birthday party is why not," said Ferguson. "You can't be trusted at events."

Norris heaved a sigh. Ferguson had invited him to his birthday party some time between the toilet-flooding debacle and the van-painting mess. But Norris had been devastated when his mom showed him the gift she had bought for him to give to Ferguson: a set of flannel pajamas and matching robe, bought at Dads and Lads, the only half-decent local place to shop for clothes in Lower Narrow Spit.

"Mom!" Norris had complained. "I can't give Ferguson *that*! Kids don't like pajamas for presents."

"Sure they do," insisted his mom, stroking the plush fabric. "You'll see."

Norris had not wanted to take any chances, so he convinced the entire class that Ferguson had secretly told him he really wanted pajamas just like Norris's for his birthday.

When Ferguson's party finally arrived, he unwrapped seventeen sets of pajamas.

"Oh, come on!" Norris said. "That was a long time ago. And anyway, I have something to put in the show. Something made by your grandfather's old fishing buddy, which makes my object extra special."

Norris was referring to McDermit's door handle that his mom had framed in their pantry.

"Who?" asked Ferguson suspiciously.

"McDermit," Norris announced.

"McDermit," repeated Ferguson, eyes widening.

"So I'm in?" asked Norris, knowing that he was in for sure.

It was Ferguson's turn to heave a sigh.

"I suppose," said Ferguson. "Come by Friday after school. That's when we'll be finished setting up."

He turned and continued on his way to Sunset Manor, life ring bumping against his sweater vest.

Interview

Norris sat in the rocker on Graeme's porch, waiting for another update. He was still insulted by Ferguson's lack of forgiveness. But Ferguson was his ticket into Sunset Manor, where Graeme was definitely up to something.

Graeme climbed the steps to his house, having fed the giant lobster at the community museum. He bent to give Fetch a scratch once he landed on the porch.

"I'm here for my update," Norris declared, rocking nowhere near Fetch's tail.

Creak, creak. Creak, creak.

"Have a look," said Graeme, eyeing the distance between Fetch's tail and the rocker nonetheless.

He reached into his pocket and unfolded the list of suspects. He had crossed off the names of those whom he had already ruled out: Allen, and now Georgia.

Norris grabbed the list and scanned it.

"You know what I think," said Norris, snapping his fingers. "You're going to run out of time, if you ask me."

"What are you talking about?!" Graeme demanded. He snatched the list back. "There're only two names left to investigate. And one of them walks by my house all the time."

"Who? Ferguson?"

"Yes, Ferguson. I saw him go by just the other day. Look, here he comes again now," Graeme said hotly.

Both boys watched as Ferguson rounded the corner and passed below Graeme's house, sweater vest and all.

"Go on, then," Norris taunted. "Investigate, Mr. Science."

"Don't forget your side of the deal," Graeme warned, and he took off down the steps. "Ferguson!" he called out.

Ferguson stopped to look up. He smiled when he saw that it was Graeme.

"Where are you headed?" Graeme asked as the two set off together.

"I'm going to play ping-pong with my granddad," Ferguson replied. He patted the paddle that was tucked into his back pocket. "Is that *Norris* on your porch?"

Both boys looked up at Graeme's house.

Norris instinctively ducked behind the cover of the lilac bush by the porch, but he was a beat too late. Still, he smiled to himself. His plan to dupe Graeme into casting suspicion upon others for the missing cactus was back on track. And whatever Graeme was planning at Sunset Manor to drive up the bidding would be doomed to fail once Norris got his foot in the door to tell everyone there that his dad was going to make sure the giant lobster *stayed* in Lower Narrow Spit.

Norris gave Fetch an ear rubby as the voices of Graeme and Ferguson faded down the street.

The next day after school, Norris dropped by his dad's office, only to discover it empty except for his grandfather's mounted trophies glaring down menacingly at Norris. He wondered how his dad could stand to work in such an unfriendly environment.

For clues to his dad's whereabouts, Norris sat down at the leather-topped desk to view the computer screen.

"*The Secret to Successful Lobster Chowder*," he read out loud. It was the title of an article his dad must have been reading.

Norris turned to the stack of printouts in the printer tray. He riffled through them.

"*Easy Lobster Chowder. Corn and Lobster Soup. Rock Lobster Bisque. Lobster Stew and You.*"

He must have been researching chowder recipes all morning, thought Norris.

But why?

Then something occurred to Norris. His dad, who had not grown up in Lower Narrow Spit, did not know anything about lobster chowders. Judging a contest was going to be a challenge, especially in front of all the locals.

Norris grabbed the paperweight on his dad's desk and twirled around in the chair to face the window. He spotted his dad moving full stride down the wharf — tie a-flapping — toward three people standing beside *Homarus II*. They were Graeme, Graeme's dad and someone who appeared to be a reporter from the city, judging by the microphone she held out and her stylish shoes.

Norris watched in fascination. Clearly, his dad was interrupting an interview. The reporter barely turned to face him as he gestured grandly toward the cannery. Then she turned back to Graeme and Graeme's dad to ask more questions while Norris's dad stood awkwardly by.

Norris's ears went pink. He looked down at the shipwreck in his hand, then back to the scene on the wharf. His dad could not jam a word in edgewise.

Norris had been shut out of conversations plenty of times, and he was certainly used to it. But seeing his dad treated in the same ill manner? Norris's stomach gave a lurch.

Any reporter should know that there were three types of people in this world: those who

worked for the newspaper; those who *bought*
the newspaper; and those who *owned a cannery
that paid for expensive advertisements so that the
newspaper company could hire reporters!*

Norris turned away from the pitiful scene.
He placed the paperweight back on his dad's
desk and slipped out so that he would not add
to his dad's embarrassment. Then he headed to
the empty playground to get his mind off things.
After soaring on the swings until the last lobster
boat had tied up at the government wharf for the
day, he heard a familiar voice that pulled him out
of his sadness.

"Norris!" his dad called from his convertible.
"I'm going to the post office. Want to come for
the ride?"

Norris jumped off and ran over to the car.
He opened the dented door and climbed in,
grateful that his dad was acting as if nothing had
happened at the wharf.

The post office, like everything else, was located on Main Street. It was an old stone building with fat brass doorknobs and a slow-moving ceiling fan that did almost nothing to change the temperature.

Mr. Cornell, the postmaster, nodded politely from behind the counter.

"I hear that the steering committee appointed you as this year's volunteer auctioneer," said Norris's dad after Mr. Cornell handed him a thick stack of cannery mail bound by an elastic band.

"You bet," said Mr. Cornell. "And that giant lobster's really going to make the bidding interesting!"

"Well, let me end the mystery for you right now," said Norris's dad, casually flipping through the envelopes. "*I'm* going to win that lobster. Guaranteed."

"I see," said Mr. Cornell, sounding slightly less friendly. "Well, then."

The ceiling fan made several slow rotations, pushing the awkward silence into the four corners of the room.

Finally, Norris chimed in.

"Dad's got a lobster festival job, too. He's going to be the judge for this year's chowder contest."

"I heard that," said Mr. Cornell, returning to his jovial self. "But I should warn you! My wife makes the best lobster chowder around."

"Is that a fact," said Norris's dad, using the same icy tone he used at the cannery. "I hope she has one or two secret ingredients up her sleeve."

"Secret ingredients," repeated Mr. Cornell, frowning. "Like what?"

"Like bacon," said Norris's dad. "Or sundried tomatoes. Maybe even goat cheese or sherry."

Mr. Cornell's mouth fell open.

"My wife," he said with deliberate care, "has been making chowder since she was tall enough to stir a pot on the stove. Chowder is made of lobster, haddock, scallops, diced potatoes, carrots, onion, butter, cream and plenty of black pepper. That's it! And you'd know that if you weren't from away!"

"I guess I'll be the judge of that," said Norris's dad curtly.

Norris traipsed after his dad out the door. They drove home together in stony silence, Norris wishing he had not come to the post office and feeling as if he had been forced to watch the reporter-on-the-wharf scene all over again.

Tricked

Two days later, Norris consoled himself while sitting in Graeme's porch rocker, waiting for his last update. As soon as Graeme finished his investigation, Norris would reveal Graeme's suspect list at school. Accusations would fly, with Norris safely standing at the sidelines, *for once* not the center for blame. And when his dad *did* win that giant lobster at the auction, he would be sure to get all the respect that he deserved.

Norris rocked back and forth until he spotted Graeme leaving Deckland's garage and picking up speed for home. Nails, Deckland's kitten, romped behind Graeme, but then trailed off to play by the whale bone.

Deckland was the last suspect on Norris's list. Graeme's investigation must be complete.

Perfect!

"Why'd you trick me?!" Graeme demanded as he sprang up the steps two at a time.

"What do you mean?" Norris asked, even though he knew exactly what was coming.

"Nails isn't your kitten! And *no one* on your list stole Ms. Penfield's cactus!"

Norris smiled.

"See! Everyone says you're smart," said Norris. "That's why I picked you."

Creak, creak. Creak, creak.

Graeme remained standing, fists clenched, shoulders pressed to his ears. But it was his look of utter disdain that really rubbed Norris the wrong way, as if to say that Norris could never hope to outsmart *him*.

Well, Norris had news for Graeme!

"Look," said Norris, dead calm. "I accidentally knocked the cactus to the floor. I tried to catch it as it fell, but it scratched me up before the flower broke off, so I had to toss the whole thing into the compost bin. I thought that if I got you to do some investigating, others might be suspected of causing its disappearance, and then I'd get off the hook. The kitten was a nice decoy, you have to admit."

Creak, creak. Creak, creak.

Graeme opened his mouth, but nothing came out.

"And it worked." Norris continued. "Because of you, there will be plenty of accusations cast about. So don't worry. You've done your part. Now all I've got to do is talk my dad into bidding high on your giant lobster."

Norris stood in triumph. He knew that there was no way Graeme would tell others about how he had been duped by the likes of Norris.

It would be far too humiliating! Still, now might be a good time to remind Graeme of his ultimate goal: a trip to Big Fish Aquarium.

Norris adjusted his ball cap.

Only, Graeme ignored the gesture. Instead, he stepped over Fetch, heaved the screen door open and let it slam shut behind him.

"Some people's kids," Norris confided to Fetch.

Fetch stood. Then he stared at Norris, ears pressed flat.

"Blink, at least," said Norris.

Fetch did not oblige.

Norris spun on his heels and headed down the stairs. He was not about to explain to a silly old dog how his plan was a beautiful thing: Norris off the hook about the cactus, a cannery trophy for his dad, and a trip to Big Fish for Graeme meant that *everyone* was going to win. Too bad Norris alone had such foresight!

It was Friday morning, the day before the lobster festival. Norris was certain that Ms. Penfield would be swinging by to pick up her cactus any minute. That meant accusations surrounding its disappearance would have to fly soon.

His thoughts about where to start were interrupted by yet another peculiar question from Ferguson during math class.

"I'm puzzled by the words 'empty' and 'nothing,'" Ferguson stated.

The fill-in teacher hesitated at the blackboard.

"You see, if something is empty, then there is nothing in it, but if someone *feels* empty, then they *feel* something, not nothing," Ferguson continued.

Norris thought his head would explode. It was then that he decided to make his sweater-vested classmate his first target. Halfway through their pop quiz, he leaned toward Ferguson.

Sensing Norris, Ferguson hunkered down over his answers.

"I'm not cheating," whispered Norris. "I've got something to tell you."

"Go away," Ferguson warned, hunkering down even more.

"Ms. Penfield's orange-flowered cactus is missing."

Ferguson tore his eyes away from his test to glance at their beloved teacher's plant collection in the window.

"I knew it! She was crazy putting *you* in charge."

"Graeme thought you might have had something to do with it," Norris whispered.

"What?!" Ferguson exclaimed, sitting bolt upright.

"Shhhhh!" others whispered from all around.

The fill-in teacher looked up, then back to her book once the silence resumed.

"Graeme's been investigating for me," Norris whispered. "He thinks it could have been Georgia or Deckland, too."

Norris clearly enunciated the names "Georgia" and "Deckland."

It worked! They both jerked their heads in his direction.

"Tests forward, please," announced their fill-in teacher upon checking the wall clock.

Papers flew past Ferguson to the front of the room.

"Is that why he walked with me the other day to Sunset Manor?" Ferguson asked in a small voice.

"Some people's kids," said Norris with a shrug, and headed out the door.

Word spread like a hurricane, flinging waves in all directions, with Mr. Science at the eye of the storm.

At recess, Norris spotted Graeme sitting alone on a bench, trying to hide behind his marine aquarium magazine to no avail, while accused classmates reproached him from all around.

"When did *you* get so sneaky?"

"How am I supposed to trust *you* ever again?"

"I thought *you* were smarter than that."

Norris waited for the angry mob to disperse. In his experience, they always did. Eventually.

He sidled up to Graeme and spoke.

"You know what I think," said Norris. "You're mad at me now, but after you spend the prize money at Big Fish Aquarium, you'll forget all about it, if you ask me."

Graeme stopped pretending to read. He slapped the covers shut, looking as if he was going to haul off and let Norris have it.

Norris backed away, then headed to the playground swings. He knew he was right: Big Fish Aquarium was one of the largest in the world.

"My turn!" Allen predictably shouted as Norris swooped past the lineup to jump on a newly vacated swing.

Norris barely heard him, for an unsettling image from yesterday came into his mind as he soared above the hostile crowd.

It was an image of Fetch.

Fetch standing guard at Graeme's door. Fetch remaining in position until Norris had retreated all the way down Graeme's stairs. Fetch unblinking as Norris made a hasty escape down Main Street.

It was as if the old dog was wise to Norris's tricks.

By the time the end-of-day school bell rang, Norris was more than ready for the happy distraction of visiting the Know the Ropes Show at Sunset Manor. He grabbed his backpack off the hook in the school's crowded hallway and patted it down. Having raided the pantry after breakfast, he was glad to discover McDermit's framed door handle still stashed inside.

When Norris arrived at the seniors' residence, it was all surprisingly familiar. He recognized the manicured green lawn cut in a precise diamond pattern, the cheerful multicolored flowerbeds and the Adirondack chairs arranged in pleasing groupings. It looked just like Norris's garden at home, and when Norris saw a familiar man waving at him from a ride-on mower, he realized it was no wonder: his family employed the same gardener.

Norris pushed open the glass double doors and went inside, eager for the opportunity to wow the crowd, the way his dad was sure to do at tomorrow's auction.

Fiasco

Norris was immediately overwhelmed. There were old people milling everywhere, some with canes, some with walkers and some with wheelchairs. The shiny floors squeaked with every step. Several televisions were blaring. And what was that fishy smell?

"Who might you be?" said a hunched man in a flannel shirt, shuffling up to Norris.

"Norris," said Norris, clutching his knapsack between himself and the flannel-shirted man.

"What?" the flannel-shirted man said, adjusting his hearing aid.

"Norris," Norris repeated louder.

"What?" the flannel-shirted man said.

"I see you made it," Ferguson said, appearing from the crowd. "This is Mr. Hastings."

"Nice to meet you," Norris said politely, still looking around for the source of the odd smell.

"This is called the common room," Ferguson explained. "We had to move the furniture to make space for the exhibit."

The couches were pushed off to the side. Card tables were lined up along one wall to support the objects on display. Above them hung a large banner with the words "Know the Ropes" written out in actual rope.

It reminded Norris of the hideous rope-framed plaster-of-paris plaque featuring lobster claws back at the community museum where he had been eavesdropping on Graeme and his treacherous plan to drive up the bidding.

Norris and Ferguson made their way over to the display after helping themselves to glasses of purple-colored punch. It left curved stains at the corners of their mouths.

"Here we are," Ferguson said proudly with a sweep of his hand.

Norris looked up and down the display. What a hodgepodge! Fishing gear all a-jumble, boat tools of every description heaped together, captains' wheels and boat nameplates fighting for wall space — and the source of the unpleasant odor: stiffened oilskins that reeked of fish bait and linseed. The air hummed as if the exhibit had washed up at low tide.

"And this is my granddad," Ferguson said, slipping his arm around an old man with wildly bushy eyebrows, a sweater vest and pants pulled up to his chest. He was about Ferguson's height.

"Nice to meet you," Ferguson's grandfather said, shaking Norris's hand.

"So what did you bring of McDermit's?" Ferguson asked.

Norris pulled out the shed-door handle from his backpack and handed it to Ferguson.

"It's a homemade door handle," Ferguson observed.

His grandfather leaned in for a better view.

"Looks like McDermit's handiwork all right," he said fondly.

"It's from McDermit's fish shed," Norris confirmed.

"You took it right off the door?" Ferguson asked, alarm creeping into his voice.

"No," Norris said dismissively. "The shed was torn down when we added our tennis court at Marshy Hope. This is all that's left."

"McDermit's fish shed is gone?" Ferguson's

grandfather asked, rubbing his stubble chin with his large knurly fingers.

"Sure," Norris said matter-of-factly. "It was old and useless and in the way."

Nobody said anything.

Ferguson's grandfather cleared his throat.

"I think I'll go get myself some punch," he said quietly.

But he did not go to the punch bowl. Instead, he lowered himself onto one of the couches that was pushed into a corner at the far end of the room and stared at nothing at all.

Ferguson thrust the framed door handle back to Norris.

"Why'd you go and say that?" Ferguson demanded.

"What?" Norris said, confused.

"Getting rid of things that are *old* and *useless* and *in the way*?!" Ferguson said. "You really know how to cheer folks up around here!"

Norris's ears went pink. But then he remembered he did have exciting news that these retired fishermen *would* appreciate.

"I can fix it," Norris said to Ferguson.

He ignored Ferguson's menacing scowl and proceeded to stand on the seat of a nearby chair. He peered down on a sea of gray heads.

"Can I please have everybody's attention?"

The din quieted, and everyone turned to face Norris.

"As you probably all know, a giant lobster has been caught in our bay and will be auctioned off during tomorrow's annual lobster festival."

A few heads nodded.

"Well, what if there are bidders from all over? That lobster could end up almost anywhere! But my dad thinks that it should stay in Lower Narrow Spit, and he's going to see to that. He promises to be the highest bidder and turn it into a trophy for our community's biggest building: the Lucky Catch Cannery!"

Norris beamed, hands on hips.

Then he looked around.

Norris, to his bewilderment, was surrounded by stunned silence.

Jaws dropped.

Nobody breathed.

Ferguson's grandfather slowly rose to his feet.

"McDermit caught a lobster like that in his day. And I was on the wharf when he hauled it in."

"I know. But it didn't end up as a trophy. Now we'll have one. Right here. In Lower Narrow Spit." Norris paused, looking to the crowd for support.

"There's no trophy because McDermit's lobster died," said Ferguson's grandfather gravely. "It was McDermit's biggest regret. McDermit told us that something that old should have been returned to the sea."

Ferguson's grandfather fixed Norris with a stony look, then sank back down.

All eyes returned to Norris. There were glares.

Norris scrambled off the chair. He had trouble swallowing, and his stomach felt as if a giant dodgeball had smacked it.

He looked for help from Ferguson. But Ferguson stood holding the front doors open. He briskly waved Norris through without another word.

The sickening feeling stayed with Norris that evening and into the next day. He had not slept at all, having tossed and turned over the fiasco at Sunset Manor, along with the recurring image of Fetch that for some reason he could not shake.

The smell of chowder did not help.

"Chunky," Norris's dad declared after dipping his spoon into the bowl belonging to one of the contestants.

The rest of the entries were lined up on a table at the community museum where the lobster festival's chowder contest was being held. The crowd of onlookers, including Georgia and Mr. Cornell's wife, stood in a semicircle and watched the judge's every move.

"Salty," Norris's dad announced, setting down his spoon to score the last bowl.

Norris's stomach gave a lurch. He clutched it, thinking he might throw up. He bolted for the door before hearing his dad announce the results of the contest.

Outside, Norris gulped the fresh air. Then he took a walk to try to clear his head.

He stopped to watch the lobster-trap-building contest on the government wharf. That reminded him of the giant lobster. He stood on the sidelines as the parade marched down Main Street, until a float bearing an enormous lobster waving hardware tools drifted past him. That reminded him of the giant lobster. He paused to watch the crowning of this year's Princess Mermaid and King Neptune, but when Graeme's little sister, Lynnette, refused to give up her crown to this year's winner and ran off with a silk cape covered in hand-sewn lobster claws, that, too, reminded him of the giant lobster.

At last, Norris wandered into the old dance hall where the lobster supper was being served and where the auction would be held right after the meal. He found a spot at one of the long tables and sat down, only to pick at his plate of food.

"Hello, Norris," said a familiar voice.

Norris looked up. It was Ms. Penfield holding her brand-new baby.

Confession

"Is this seat taken?" Ms. Penfield asked kindly.

"No," said Norris, and he shoved over on the bench to make room.

On top of everything else, Norris could not escape the matter of the broken orange-flowered cactus, the accident that had caused everything else to unfold so miserably.

By now, she would have discovered that it was missing.

Things could not get worse.

Perhaps it was time to turn things around.

Perhaps it was time for the truth.

"I have something to tell you," Norris said, ears turning the same color as the boiled lobster on his plate. "Your cactus isn't missing. I broke the flower, then turned the parts into compost. The whole thing was an accident."

"I see," Ms. Penfield said. "I did hear rumors at the playground when I went to pick it up after school." She paused to consider Norris. "I think you are very brave to confess."

Norris dared to look at his teacher. She gave him a pat on the shoulder, then turned to her baby.

"You're not mad?" Norris asked.

"To tell you the truth, Norris, I have someone far more important to take care of than my silly old plant collection."

She stroked her sleeping baby's cheek.

Norris sighed with relief, but it was short-lived.

"May I have everyone's attention?" Mr. Cornell called out from the podium at the far end of the dance hall. "If you're finished your supper, would you please move to the seats by the stage, because we are about to begin our final event, Lower Narrow Spit's annual lobster festival auction."

Someone waved to Norris from the front row.

It was Norris's dad, saving Norris a seat.

Norris was filled with dread. He slowly made his way over to his dad, walking past the reporters and camera operators milling along the side of the room. It was one thing to watch his dad from afar being humiliated by a reporter. It was going to be quite another to sit right at his side while being humiliated in front of an entire television crew.

Norris braved a quick survey of the crowd. He caught a fleeting view of his mom, busily overseeing the supper cleanup while everyone else was still grabbing seats. Graeme and his dad were three rows back. Directly behind Norris, Ms. Carrington was sitting with her son, Allen, who had rolled up an auction program to fire spitballs. Nearby, Ms. Penfield was holding her baby, surrounded by some of Ferguson's gushing sisters. Mr. Cornell's wife and Georgia were sitting at the back, neither of them looking as if they had won the lobster chowder contest. Deckland was standing at the rear, still wearing his plastic lobster bib from supper. And across the room was a group from Sunset Manor, including Ferguson, Ferguson's grandfather and Mr. Hastings, all wearing their trademark sweater vests.

It was, Norris realized grimly, the entire town.

Norris muffled a groan. He sat staring at the stage where various items to be auctioned off were on display: a free membership to the curling rink; a crate of canned lobster packed on ice; knitted fisherman's sweaters; a gift basket from the drugstore; a voucher for lunch for two at the Chinese restaurant; gardening tools; homemade pies; crafts made by residents at Sunset Manor; and, of course, taking center stage, the monster lobster staring out from its tank.

Mr. Cornell adjusted the mic at the podium. Mr. Quackenbush, the town's mayor, stood behind him to assist with the bidding.

A hush filled the room. Norris's heart pounded in his ears.

"Good evening and welcome," boomed Mr. Cornell. "Let's waste no time and get straight to the bidding. First up, a crate of the finest canned lobster in the world, generously donated by Lower Narrow Spit's very own cannery."

"That's Lucky Catch," added Norris's dad. He half stood and waved to the crowd, but the applause was fleeting. Norris cringed.

"Now, who wants to start the opening bid?" asked Mr. Cornell jovially.

Norris wondered how much more painful suspense he could take.

"When is the bidding for the giant lobster going to happen?" he whispered to his dad.

"It won't be bid on until the end, but don't you worry. That lobster's mine."

Norris was worried, all right.

"Hey, bada-bada-bada," called Mr. Cornell as bids started to roll in.

The auction went on and on, one item of inconsequence selling after another. Slowly, slowly the stage grew bare around the giant lobster.

And then there was just the giant lobster, perfect for the cannery, or so his dad thought.

"Well, ladies and gentlemen. That concludes Lower Narrow Spit's annual lobster festival auction. We've got nothing left to sell … no, wait. What's this?" joked Mr. Cornell, turning to the giant crustacean in mock amazement.

The crowd laughed at his antics.

Norris picked at a festering scab.

"Do I have an opening bid?" asked Mr. Cornell, looking everywhere except in the direction of Norris's dad.

Norris's dad confidently held up his paddle and nodded to the cameras.

"Hey, bada-bada-bada," droned Mr. Cornell. "Hey, bada-bada-bada."

Norris struggled to breathe. Then he heard a commotion behind him.

"We have a second bidder!" announced Mr. Cornell in surprise.

Victory

Both Norris and his dad wheeled around to see who would dare outbid them. They did not recognize the stranger sitting beside Graeme. He was wearing a Big Fish Aquarium shirt with the word "Staff" printed on his chest.

Graeme beamed with defiance at Norris. Clearly, he had lured the Big Fish man to Lower Narrow Spit to ensure a bidding war.

But unknown to Graeme, his underhanded scheme gave Norris's dad room for a narrow escape.

"Hey, bada-bada-bada," called Mr. Cornell, perking up. "Hey, bada-bada-bada."

Norris's dad rammed his paddle into the air. "Hey, bada-bada-bada. Hey, bada-bada-bada."

The Big Fish man shot his paddle up in retaliation.

"Hey, bada-bada-bada. Hey, bada-bada-bada."

Back and forth. Back and forth. The bids getting higher and higher. Norris's dad growing ever more frustrated in his seat. Suddenly, he leaned over to Norris.

"Watch. This is how you earn respect, even if you *aren't* from around here."

Then Norris's dad shouted to Mr. Cornell. "Let's put an end to this silliness! I'll give you *double* what the last bidder gave!"

The crowd gasped.

Norris turned to the audience. Instead of respect, all he saw were familiar faces filled with scorn.

The Big Fish man hesitated, then signaled to

the auctioneer that he was still in the game. But even from where he sat, Norris could see that the stranger's paddle was shaking.

The crowd leaned forward in their seats. All eyes turned to Norris's dad.

Norris's dad stared straight ahead. Norris looked up at his dad, then back at the stranger bidding against them, then to his dad again.

Nobody breathed. Would Norris's dad give up? Was that possible?

"Hey, bada-bada-bada. Hey, bada-bada-bada."

Norris's dad slowly raised his paddle, electrifying the crowd.

Everyone shifted in their seats, then turned to the stranger.

The Big Fish man slumped his shoulders and laid his paddle on his lap. Graeme whispered something to him. The stranger sadly stared at his feet.

Graeme put his head in his hands.

And Norris's stomach reeled violently. His dad was poised to win.

"Now hold your horses. That lobster's not sold yet!" a new voice shouted from the crowd. "It's our turn to join the bidding!"

Norris spun around. It was Ferguson's grandfather surrounded by his Sunset Manor cronies.

The old man clutched a paddle in his giant knurly fist and thrust it into the air. The reporters and camera operators adjusted their equipment to record the stunning turn of events.

"Something that's survived so long deserves to be set free," announced Ferguson's grandfather, speaking grandly to the cameras. "That's what McDermit always told us."

"So we've pooled our money, and we're going to bid in his memory!" Ferguson added, waving a wad of money in the air as proof.

The audience murmured their approval.

Norris wanted to crawl under a rock.

Mr. Cornell started up again.

"Hey, bada-bada-bada. Hey, bada-bada-bada."

Norris's dad kept his back to the audience. He raised his paddle and nodded deliberately at Mr. Cornell.

The audience muttered unhappily.

"Hey, bada-bada-bada. Hey, bada-bada-bada."

Ferguson's grandfather jabbed the air with his paddle.

The audience whooped and stomped their feet.

"Hey, bada-bada-bada. Hey, bada-bada-bada."

Norris's dad responded with his paddle thrust high for all to see.

The audience made grumpy noises.

"Hey, bada-bada-bada. Hey, bada-bada-bada," said Mr. Cornell, tugging at his collar.

The old man formed a huddle with his buddies, along with Ferguson. Ferguson looked grim. The huddle cleared, then Ferguson's grandfather raised his paddle again. Only this time, he seemed to be looking defeat in the eye, as if this was the last bid that Sunset Manor could manage.

The audience saw that look. They all held their breath.

Norris saw that look, too. He swallowed hard, knowing that the whole town was about to turn on his dad forever.

Norris's dad held up his paddle one last time with the confidence of the owner of the town's only cannery.

"Hey, bada-bada-bada," said Mr. Cornell, mustering no enthusiasm whatsoever.

Ferguson's grandfather cursed a blue streak, then plunked down in his seat. His buddies reached over from their chairs to thump his back in sympathy. Ferguson gave him a hug.

"Sold to the highest bidder," announced Mr. Cornell dully. "I'm sure this giant lobster will make a fine trophy for the cannery, to be enjoyed by the folks of Lower Narrow Spit for years and years to come."

"I won!" exclaimed Norris's dad.

Only Norris and everyone else in the dance hall knew just how badly he had lost.

Norris's dad stood and cleared his throat. He began making his way to the podium to say a few words, having paid a princely sum for his trophy.

And then, in a flash of brilliance, Norris saw what to do.

He bolted from his chair and scooted past his dad to the podium. He quickly bent the microphone down to his height.

"I want everyone to know," announced Norris, rushing his words, "that my dad has decided to set the giant lobster free!"

Norris's dad froze in mid-stride. He sputtered, and his mouth stuck half open.

Graeme looked at Norris in disbelief.

Norris signaled Graeme with a quick snap of his fingers: get on with it!

Graeme's look of recognition replaced his appearance of defeat.

"Hear, hear!" Graeme exclaimed to the confused audience. He jumped up and began to clap.

From across the room, Ferguson stood to join the solitary clapper.

The crowd hesitated briefly, a beat behind Graeme and Ferguson, two beats behind Norris. Then they roared their applause in a standing ovation.

Norris's dad turned to the audience. His furious look gave way to surprise, then to a flattered smile. Norris stepped away from the microphone to make room for his dad at the podium. His dad grabbed Norris's hand, and the two faced the cheering crowd, holding their arms up in victory.

"Some people's kids!" Norris's dad shouted but with pride into Norris's ear during the deafening applause.

Release

It was early morning and still dark out when
Norris's dad woke him up by turning on his
bronze captain's wheel lamp.

"Be sure to keep quiet," he whispered. "Your
mom's exhausted with all her steering-committee
work."

Norris nodded. He stretched before getting
up and remembered that he had dreamed of
Fetch. Only this time, Fetch had been relaxing on
Graeme's porch in his usual sprawled position by
the rocker, tail thumping contentedly now and then.

"Steak and eggs!" Norris exclaimed with delight, sitting down to breakfast as his dad slid a plate in front of him.

"Big day ahead," Norris's dad replied.

Norris was famished. He smothered everything in ketchup and dug right in.

As Norris chewed, he turned to survey the mountain of gear already stashed at the back door: survival suits, sou'westers, life jackets, rubber boots, tripods and camera equipment.

Norris's dad checked his watch.

"Better get going," he announced, and Norris pushed his steak bone to the side of his plate.

They piled their yacht-store belongings into the convertible with the dent that was scheduled for repair tomorrow, then drove down to the government wharf. It was still dark, but less so. They hurried when they heard the rumbling of a lobster boat diesel engine.

"You weren't going to leave without us, were you, Swinimer?" Norris's dad called down from the wharf.

"Just warming up the boat," said Graeme's dad. "Climb aboard."

The rest of the crew were already on the boat: Graeme, the Big Fish man from the aquarium, Ferguson, Ferguson's grandfather and Mr. Hastings. The giant lobster, which had been loaded onto *Homarus II* the night before, was safely in the hold.

"You know what I think," said Norris's dad after they settled in the stern and he handed the camera to Norris. "My release of this lobster will make a splendid photograph for the cannery."

The passengers nodded amicably.

"What?" Mr. Hastings asked, tugging at his hearing aid.

The sun peeked above the horizon.

"Would you look at that!" exclaimed Norris as pinks and oranges burned across the sky.

He raised his camera to take a picture.

"Haven't you ever seen the sunrise from a boat?" Graeme asked, pushing the stern off the wharf with the gaffing pole after *Homarus II* dropped her lines.

"No," said Norris. "Dad says there's no need. I'm going to run the cannery when I grow up."

He turned to face the receding silhouette of Lower Narrow Spit: the old dance hall, the curling rink, the bank, the drugstore, the post office, the hardware store, the minimart, the community museum, the diner that sold famous Chinese takeout with special lobster sauce and, most imposing of all, the enormous aluminum-clad building that he would one day own.

Graeme went to chat at the wheel, and Norris held the camera so that he could take a photograph of himself with the whole town as a backdrop. He snapped the picture, which he would later print and frame for his bedroom.

"Oh. Before I forget," Norris said to Graeme as they slowed down to where Graeme's dad thought was a good spot to release the giant lobster.

Norris reached into his pocket and pulled out a steak bone wrapped in a plastic bag. He handed it to Graeme while Ferguson looked on, perplexed.

"For Fetch," Norris explained, and that made his classmates smile.

Acknowledgments

I did not grow up in a lobster community, so when I was invited on a book tour to Cape Breton, Nova Scotia, I leaped at the chance. Views from the twisty, cliff-hugging roads of the Cabot Trail were far grander than any tourist photograph could ever hope to capture. Unfolding before me between school visits were extraordinary places like Wreck Cove, Aspy Bay and Cape North. In every community, both wooden curve-topped traps and the more modern square wire-mesh traps were stacked high at the wharves. Striped marker buoys piled next to the traps were rocked by gusting winds. Lobster boats splashed in primary colors were straining against their mooring lines behind gigantic breakwaters, as if impatiently waiting for the lobster season to begin. And all the while, eagles swooped overhead and road signs warned of moose crossings.

Thank you to Christine Thomson and Tara MacNeil, of the Cape Breton Regional Library in Sydney, Nova Scotia, who made that tour so memorable.

I would also like to thank my editor, Sheila Barry, for her insightful comments, and for sharing her family's lobster chowder recipe with me, and to Peter Kerrin for his unwavering support, even during the awkward early drafts, which I read out loud to him during our long drives between Nova Scotia and Maine.

One more thing. I bought a souvenir from one of the many craft shops along the North Shore of the Cabot Trail. It was a large metal cutout of a flounder — a type of fish that has both eyes on one side of its head. With such an unmatched perspective, I wondered how a flounder would see things? And, when I toured the lobster communities, I wondered the same thing about its people. I hope I got it right.

Enjoy more chapter books from Kids Can Press!

**Jasper John Dooley:
Star of the Week**
HCJ 978-1-55453-578-1

Lower the Trap
HCJ 978-1-55453-576-7

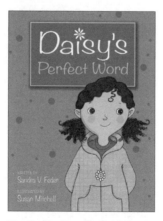

Daisy's Perfect Word
HCJ 978-1-55453-645-0